BOOK 2 OF THE ALTERATIONS TRILOGY

GAME CHANGER

BOOKS BY JANE SUEN

Children of the Future
Flowers in December

THE ALTERATIONS TRILOGY SERIES
Alterations
Game Changer

SHORT STORIES
Beginnings and Endings: A Selection of Short Stories

BOOK 2 OF THE ALTERATIONS TRILOGY

GAME CHANGER

JANE SUEN

GAME CHANGER: Book 2 of the Alterations Trilogy

Jane Suen books are available for order through Ingram Press Catalogues

www.janesuen.com

Printed in the United States of America

First Printing: June 2018

ISBN: 978-1-7323873-1-7

Ebook ISBN: 978-1-7323873-0-0

For my loved ones.

Chapter 1
DR. KITE

One year, three months and two days after the fire destroyed Dr. Kite's warehouse.

Her voice reached his ears before he saw her. She was speaking, the words punctuated by soft laughter. What drew him closer, full of curiosity? Was it her tone, pleasant but firm? Perhaps he sensed it—her vitality, freshness, and energy. Before he realized it, he had walked down the grocery aisle to her sample meal kiosk.

She had an audience, watching as she dipped her spoon in a pot of chili simmering on an electric burner and divvied small portions into bite-sized paper cups on the counter. The finishing touch, a tiny plastic spoon, decorated each cup.

He stayed beyond the edge of the crowd, watching as she continued to talk, all the while doling out the samples. He was right about her. Young. Early twenties. Her long hair swept back in a ponytail.

She must have felt him staring at her as she held up a

sample of chili, scanning the crowd for volunteers willing to try it. Suddenly, she looked straight at him, her beautiful blue eyes innocent and wide.

He met her gaze before casting his eyes down. He looked at his rumpled pants, still full of creases from the day before, and the worn brown belt with the dull buckle at his waist, his crinkled, blue cotton shirt barely tucked in. Disgusted with himself, he quietly retreated, cursing his appearance, wishing he could change her first impression of him.

Chapter 2
ELLEN

When Ellen missed her period, she dismissed it. *It's all this stress and trauma*, she thought. Sure, she had experienced irregularities in the past when her weight yo-yoed. She had chalked it up to another one and never gave it another thought. But, one month later, when her period didn't return, she couldn't help worrying. A suppressed memory surfaced of the day when she stepped into the little shop, the one with the Alterations sign. She stiffened, thinking, *What if the microchip has something to do with this?*

After work on Friday, she stopped at a drugstore. Overwhelmed by the choices available, she had no idea which one was better. She finally grabbed two pregnancy test kits and bought both, a pee-on-a-stick and a digital test kit.

Ellen waited until Saturday morning when she could take her time and not rush it. Waking up, she took the kits to the bathroom. She sat on the toilet lid, holding the first box in her hand, turning it over, rotating the sides to read each word. Tearing off the end tabs, Ellen pulled out the kit and the pregnancy test instruction. She unfolded the slip of paper, flattening and smoothing the creases on her lap. It had pictures explaining the results. A single line meant negative; double lines meant a positive test.

She held the test stick with care, pinching the handle end with two fingers. *Let's get this over with,* she prodded herself. She bent over the open toilet, slowly releasing the first stream of morning urine. She shoved the stick in its path, midstream.

Ellen averted her eyes from the stick. She resisted the urge to stare at it on the counter, focusing instead on the nearby LED alarm clock. She cursed, wishing she had a watch with a moving second hand, as she waited for the red numbers to change. Time appeared to stand still meanwhile her emotions were churning inside her. *What if there's something wrong with the display?*

Finally, when the results were ready, she looked. She bent closer, peering at the double lines. "Oh my God!" gasped Ellen, her mouth dropping open.

She blinked. Thoughts swirled in her head. How can this be? Me, a mother? I lost weight, but I'm gaining something else—a baby!

Ellen reached for the digital pregnancy test. Ripping open the package, she removed the test strip from the wrapper and peed on the absorbent tip. This time she set the timer on her cell phone and watched the countdown, waiting until one word appeared on the screen—*Pregnant.*

Chapter 3
DR. KITE

The sound of the waves soothed him. An endless loop of incoming water crashing on the shore, retreating from the sand, rolling back in the ocean, leaving frothy bubbles in its path.

He closed his eyes behind the dark sunglasses. He lay on the sand, a towel beneath him, in a secluded area on the beach. He was safe here, far away from the busy madness of the city. Here, he'd recoup.

Kite ceased to care about his appearance after the warehouse fire took away all he had worked so hard to build—the microchips and experimental data. The fire also took away his dark secrets, hidden from plain view—the evidence of experiments gone bad, unknowing human subjects picked up by the taxis trawling the city streets from the previous night, later implanted with his microchips. Everything. Gone.

He left the city, escaping to the coast, to this small town. He no longer cared about himself, or anything, for that matter. Having been raised by strict parents, Kite had agonized over the loss. He had disappointed them, let them down after all they had sacrificed for him. A total failure.

He had applied a thin layer of sunscreen. Under the powerful rays, the sunscreen softened and melted, blending with his sweat and burning his eyes. Picking up the towel, he hastily wiped the cloth across his damp brow.

His dreams of fame and fortune crushed, he'd retreated to this hideaway to lick his wounds. And lick he did, letting himself go in the process. He knew he looked terrible, but he hadn't cared—until today.

Chapter 4
GIGI

The breeze rustled the leaves on the trees. Gigi felt a slight caress, a light touch. Standing on the porch, Gigi took in the beauty of the land—the vast expanse, the faraway mountains, majestic and dignified, capped with snow.

She had Rex to thank. He brought her here, away from the city, where time seemed to stand still. The world beyond ceased to exist.

The sound of an ax splitting wood interrupted her thoughts. Methodical, rhythmic, like background noise. Subtle, not intrusive. She turned toward the back of the cabin, walking the worn path.

"Rex!" she shouted above the sound of the chopping, adding an urgency in her voice as her steps quickened.

As she rounded the corner, Rex came into view, dressed in a plaid shirt, jeans, and work gloves. Her heart raced as she laid her eyes on him. *Her man.*

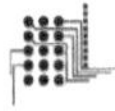

It had been three months, and two days since the morning she woke up next to Rex. The day their relationship took a new turn. It had started like any other day. He'd caught her by surprise. Okay, that part was romantic. They were having breakfast. She had picked up the napkin to wipe her mouth, and something fell out, making a soft noise as it flickered on the floor, brushing her foot before landing. She had stooped down to pick it up, and there they were—the two tickets.

Before she had a chance to say anything, Rex knelt down beside her. He was all solemn and serious. Holding her hand, he asked her to go away with him on this trip.

It seemed like Gigi had known him forever. They had been best friends for years, and roommates. Countless times they had helped each other out. She had cried on his shoulder and he'd always been there to comfort her. They had both dated other people, and boyfriends and girlfriends came and went. They stayed together as friends through thick and thin, sharing laughter and tears.

Gigi had looked at Rex, her eyes moist. "Do you remember when I had the nightmares?"

Rex nodded. "But the nightmares are gone now. You're safe."

During the ordeal with her illness, the nightmares that haunted her, the crash that came close to taking her life, Gigi had turned to Rex. Afterward, they became lovers.

But he wasn't done yet. He had another surprise for Gigi. He handed her an envelope.

"What's this?" said Gigi as she opened it, pulling out the reservation to the place he had rented. The brochure depicted enticing pictures of the mountains, a cabin with a creek running beside it, wild animals, and a spectacular sunrise. She could almost feel the breeze, suck in the crisp, clean air, see the wildlife, hear the trickle of water in the babbling brook. She squealed, excitement shining in her eyes. "I feel like I won the lottery!"

At last, they were here. All ten delicious days in their paradise, their piece of heaven. This place was indescribably beautiful, more than the photos had promised.

As she strode toward Rex, Gigi made a mental note to tell him how much she loved it here, with him. Could it be any more perfect? She was grateful. "Rex," she shouted, as she got closer to him.

He looked up, a smile spreading to his eyes.

"There's a message in the inbox." Stopping, she added, "I think you'll want to see it."

Chapter 5
GIGI

Rex put the ax down on the ground, turning the blade away. He faced Gigi, arms outstretched, a boyish grin on his face. "Come here, where's my morning hug?"

"Who are you, Paul Bunyan?"

He threw back his head, laughing heartily, as the wind gently blew his shoulder-length locks. "I'll show you," he said, giving a swagger and throwing her his best charming smile.

She wasn't averse to his appeal, his awkward charm, irresistible and goofy. Gigi grinned, a bit out of breath as she approached, angling her body as she sought the hug.

"Hi, beautiful!" he said, wrapping his arms around her.

"You're up early."

"Hmm, you know what's the best thing in the morning next to coffee?"

"Me!"

Rex pretended to be bewildered, as boisterous laughter escaped his lips.

"Well." Gigi pouted, then blew him a kiss. "That's all you're going to get." She threw him a wink, gave an exaggerated shrug of her shoulders, and turned to leave.

In a few bounds, Rex reached her, wrapping his arms around her again, pulling her back. "Oh no, you don't! I'm not going to let you go so easily."

Turning her head and pushing his arms away in a playful shove, Gigi giggled. "Who says I'm an easy catch!"

"You are the best catch of all, and I've been fishing for a long time," whispered Rex as he buried his face in her thick, luxurious hair, inhaling the fresh scent of her lavender shampoo and a whiff of gardenia.

Gigi gave a wriggle and tugged at his arm, but she was held in a firm embrace. "Let me go."

"I'll never let you go," said Rex. His voice turned serious as he whispered, "You know this."

"I like it," said Gigi.

"Like what?"

"The way you are, everything about you."

"Huh—"

"I like you." Gigi reached to pull his head closer as she looked into his eyes and pressed her lips to his. "And I love you."

"Forever and ever?"

"And you?" she said, before pulling back to search his face. She wanted to hear his response. "And do you promise to love me always?"

"As long as we both shall live." He slipped one hand down her side, reaching to take hers, pulling her toward a large log. "My lady, please sit."

"My lord," she breathed out as she daintily stepped around the log and found a place to sit.

Rex scooted next to her, sitting close enough to feel the shiver run through her body. Picking up the jacket he'd thrown across the log, he draped it across her shoulders.

They sat in silence, enjoying the scenery.

"Look how beautiful this place is. It's God's country," said Rex, nudging Gigi.

"So pristine, untouched."

"Breathtaking."

"You know what the best part is? I'm here to enjoy it with you."

"It wouldn't be the same without you," said Rex. He sat there, content. He'd be happy to stay for more than ten days, for as long as they could.

"You know, Rex?"

"What Gigi?"

"All the stuff, the bad stuff happening to me over a year ago . . ." She paused, frowning as her eyes narrowed, "I tried to block it out and forget it. It's like, sometimes I wonder if it even happened."

"It's all in the past," said Rex, turning to plant a soothing kiss on her forehead. "You don't have to relive those nightmares anymore. Forget it."

"But something good came out of it," Gigi reminded him. "If we hadn't gone through it all together, we probably wouldn't be here now." She moved her hand, touching his thumb, wrapping her fingers around it.

He pulled his thumb back. He laughed as Gigi kept her

grip on it, starting a playful tug-of-war, back and forth.

"We've had some tough times, but you are a survivor. Remember this." Rex clasped her chin with his free hand, raising her upturned face to his before planting a kiss on her trembling lips.

"Don't stop."

He kissed her until he felt the trembling subside. He turned his face, kissing the concave roundness of her palm, moving his attention to her slender fingers and dainty wrist.

"Rex, do you know how many bones are in our hands?"

"No clue."

"I looked it up once, about twenty-seven." She stretched her hands out.

He pressed her hand, gently rubbing it.

Gigi grabbed his wrist, playfully running her slim fingers down the length of his palm.

"Ooh, it tickles."

"I thought so," she said, laughing. "I can think of some other places to tickle . . ."

Gigi gave way to this playfulness, choosing not to mention the email again, preferring not to let anything ruin this happy moment as she wriggled and poked her finger in the ticklish parts of his sides.

Chapter 6
DR. KITE

How many months had it been since the fire destroyed his warehouse? More than fifteen months—a year and three months and two days plus.

Defeated, he'd left the city. For a long time, he stayed in isolation, imprisoning himself in his cheap apartment in the coastal town. As the weeks turned into months, he descended into despair mixed with a plentiful dose of self-pity.

The times he went out, he'd walk to the grocery store. A quick trip a couple of blocks away. Once there, he'd grab the items and throw them in the cart, following the same routine and route in the store. He barely looked up to see where he was going, or to view who was shopping or to dawdle and check out any new items.

Today was different. Kite had a secret agenda and headed straight to the food sample kiosk where he had watched *her* the other day, the one with the baby-blue eyes luring customers to her samples. She had sure lured him.

Today, little paper cups filled with cheesecake dotted the counter.

He reached out, hiding his disappointment at the sight of the matronly woman with old-fashioned glasses perched on her nose. He grabbed the cup closest to him. He feigned interest, conjuring the smooth, rich taste of the heavy cream, savoring each bite. Well, in this case, one bite.

He crushed the bottom of the thin paper cup, fingers tapping as his head tilted back, mouth opening to receive the piece of cake.

"Sir! Would you like to try our newest flavor of cheesecake?"

Stopping in mid-air, he said, "I've got it."

"No, sir, what you got was last year's flavor—strawberry cheesecake," said the woman, vehemently shaking her head. "You have to try the new flavor, blackberry swirl cheesecake." She pointed to a row of cups.

"Huh?" he managed as he shook the morsel in his mouth.

She smiled as she handed him another one. "You're going to like this."

He grabbed it and plopped in the second piece of cake, grimacing at the sugary overload and sudden dryness in his mouth. "You got anything to drink?"

Twisting the cap off of a bottled drink, she filled another paper cup. "Fizzy tangerine is all I've got."

He drank it in a quick gulp and tossed the cup in the waste can full of other paper cups. He snatched a napkin from a caddy filled with spoons and forks to wipe his face. He took another look at the woman, thinking, *too bad it's not her.*

"You like it?"

He managed a weak smile. "Do you do this every day?"

"Me? Naw, two times a week, occasionally three. I'm here Mondays and Wednesdays."

"I was here yesterday, but I saw another girl. Oh, um . . . what was her name?"

"Tiffany. She's our new girl here. Tuesdays and Fridays."

"So the two of you do this?"

"We had another person, but she'd quit, so they hired Tiffany."

He hid his glee behind his smile as he turned to leave. *Two more days until Friday.*

Chapter 7
LILLY

The music blasting from the alarm clock abruptly woke her. Lilly groaned and settled back under the covers, at first ignoring the sound. Her hand slammed down on the snooze button; the room stilled again.

She lay on the pillow, letting her thoughts wander. She wasn't one to run away from anything. Not even during a personal crisis like a divorce. She took it on like a thankless job, distasteful but necessary, something to get over as quickly as possible. Today she had a decision to make.

Rolling on her side, she glimpsed the framed photo on the table next to her bed. An exclusive piece of real estate, as some would say. Looking at it for the umpteenth time, Lilly saw herself, the little girl standing between her parents, wearing the one well-worn dress she had which her mother insisted she put on. Her hair was scraggly, a long time between haircuts. But the look of the little girl's face said it all. Defiant, tough. Bearing the scars of her short life.

"That's my girl," she said, looking at the photo. The

child she was. Captured on film. Lilly never had an easy life; everything she'd ever wanted she worked hard to get. Her father wished for a boy and showed his disappointment when she burst out into the world. He even wanted to name her Sam or some less-feminine variation of Samantha. But his wife wouldn't hear of it. She insisted on naming her baby. For once, she had her way.

She recalled the story her mother told about her birth certificate. The nurse in the hospital had asked her mother for the baby's name as she filled out the form for the birth certificate. Her mother said, "Lily," but when the nurse asked to confirm this, her mother, exhausted and weakened from the delivery, struggled to reply, "You know, it rhymes with Billy." So the nurse wrote down "Lilly" on the form next to her name.

Growing up, her father treated her like a boy—the boy he never had. She wanted to please him, and even dressed up as a boy and acted like a tomboy. He wasn't cruel to her, but he was severe, keeping a belt handy, which he had no qualms about using. Ever mindful of it, Lilly acted out her rebelliousness when she was with friends, but toned it down when she came home. She learned how to survive, avoiding a beating whenever she could.

Chapter 8
ELLEN

Ellen tapped the tips of her crimson, manicured nails on the notepad as she scrutinized the schedule, seeing it was tight but workable. She smiled and looked a short distance across the room to the closed door of her boss's office—her *new* boss, Andrew Capstone. *Her dream job.* After years of working for the same company, she finally got the nerve to look elsewhere.

She told herself she had an extra mouth to feed now, to care for a baby. Somehow, this gave her the strength she never had before, the final push to leave the place where she'd been working in the administrative pool.

The transformation shocked even her. She became a tigress in a man's world, competing for the lofty position she longed to have.

When she submitted her resume for the executive assistant to the director position at dEsign+, it wasn't an empty title. It had the salary to match. *Her* job, she fiercely reminded herself the day they called her to set up the interview. She bought a new outfit and had her hair and nails done.

Ellen strode into the interview room like a queen, like she owned the place, like she already had the position. And she knew, instantly and without a doubt, she had their attention and a chance at her dream job.

At the end of the interview, the director rushed up to shake her hand. She rewarded him with a cool and confident smile before she walked out.

Later in the day, the phone rang. The woman from HR said, "We'd like to offer you the job." She quoted the stated salary plus a bonus of 10 percent.

Ellen was elated, momentarily at a loss for words at the offer and a generous bonus above the industry average.

"Do you accept?"

"Yes. When do I start?"

"You can negotiate the date with your new boss, Andrew Capstone."

New boss. The words thrilled her.

He called her unexpectedly later that afternoon to congratulate her. They negotiated a good starting date. She was ready to go now but didn't say it. He wanted her sooner than later. She pushed for a later date with the excuse that she needed to take some time to wrap up the work she was doing, to leave on a good note. They agreed on the first of the following month—a Monday—which was fifteen days away.

She submitted an adequate notice to her company, giving the date of resignation. She proceeded to get herself ready for the new job in the meantime, meeting with Mr. Capstone next week to go over some preliminary items.

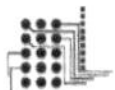

They met at the cafe across the street from the office. He had insisted on taking Ellen out to lunch to discuss the job.

"Looking forward to you coming on board, Ellen."

"Mr. Capstone," she blurted out, but he waved his hand.

"Call me Andy," he said.

Sitting next to him, Ellen had a chance to observe him close up. He appeared to be younger than she thought. She scrutinized him discreetly, taking an extra few seconds to study his face. She liked a man with salt and pepper hair—a full head of hair, no less. He looked distinguished. He appeared impeccably dressed, comfortable even in a shirt and tie.

"We've had a slew of executive assistants in the past few months who haven't worked out, and I'm hoping you'll be the one to stay."

Ellen gulped. Fidgeting in her seat, taking a sip of water, she bought some time to think. "I have no intention of leaving any time soon."

He laughed. "I'm pulling your leg. The prior occupant of your office went on maternity leave." He paused, leaning closer. "So we got temps from the agency, and they sent a different girl each week."

"Oh," Ellen said, letting out a sigh of relief. "I can't imagine how crazy it must have been."

"We managed somehow, but I'm so glad things will be going back to normal now that you're here."

Ellen raised her eyebrow. "What about the girl, the one on maternity leave . . . isn't she coming back?"

"She changed her mind after the baby. You got her job, but not exactly."

"What do you mean?"

"We upscaled it and expanded the role."

"Sir, I'll do my best," she managed to say with a brave smile, wondering if she'd have a mess to clean up.

"I'm sure you'll have a lot of questions. Speak up. I won't bite."

"I do have a question. I have a baby—well, she's a few months old now. My mother helps take care of her while I'm working." She exhaled and tucked her hair back. "Would you expect me to work late?"

He looked at her, taking time to assimilate the new information before he answered. "I may at times, depending on our deadlines. Would it be a problem?"

She thought it over. "My baby comes first. But if you need me to stay late, I'll need a heads-up and enough time to make arrangements."

"I thought your mother is taking care of her?"

"Well yes, but it's presumptive and unfair to expect her to drop everything in her life and revolve her schedule around me."

"Quite right."

"She has her own life, and I can't blame her."

"When the time comes, we'll work it out."

"Thanks," she said, relieved this was going well.

After lunch, they went back to the company for a quick tour. Ellen's new office was catty-corner from the enormous corner room of her boss. Hers was small, but enough.

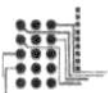

When Ellen arrived on the first day, a shiny new plate on her door bore her name and title emblazoned on copper: Ellen Fulbright, Executive Assistant to the Director. It caught her attention. She touched it with her fingertip, feeling the solid substance, admiring it.

With her hand on the doorknob, Ellen paused for a moment. Opening the door, a huge bouquet of fresh flowers on her desk greeted her. The delicate scent, the pastel colors cast in the sea of slender green stalks, delighted her senses.

She pressed her back to the closed door, soaking it in as she surveyed the scene. Someone had cleaned the desk and placed new office supplies beside the computer—a pen holder, file caddy, portfolio, stack of paper pads, shiny pens, pencils, clips. Pulling out the top drawer of her desk, she saw the smaller items in an organizer. A first aid kit tucked in the back of her drawer caught her attention. "Oh." She let out a sigh as her lips parted in a smile.

Chapter 9
GIGI

She peered in the mirror. No trace of lines around her eyes. Funny how her face was still flawless with no signs of aging. Other women spent fortunes on creams or potions to turn back Father Time, even for a few hours. Others went under the knife for a more lasting effect. She used to laugh at how much money they threw away, chasing after one promise or another. Gigi would have none of it; she didn't need to.

Gigi gently tugged at her skin, stretching it, releasing it, and then watching as it relaxed back to its original position. What she feared hadn't happened—her first line. But her relief now lacked the satisfying pretentiousness she exhibited before, although she still laughed it off, saying she had good genes.

As her friends despaired over each new wrinkle, she had kept her thoughts quietly to herself. But it didn't erase the fact she was insensitive to her friends' fears of aging.

But, after surviving the car accident, something changed inside her. Before, she had focused on her appearance—a perfect appearance. Afterward, it didn't seem to matter as much. She moved beyond it, past the fixation on the superficial part of her, her flawless skin and great beauty, shifting to the inner part of her being. Gigi sought out happiness from other things in life, things that mattered.

The car accident. She tried not to think of it, not to relive it. It still terrified her, and she made a considerable effort to avoid that spot on the road, finding detours, taking other routes instead.

In an instant, her life almost snatched away. She thought about what she would have left behind, the people she loved, memories to be created. A life not lived. She would have regretted that.

Gigi was grateful, for she had a second chance now, and she was determined to live her life fully, to love like she never loved before, to live each day like the gift it was. It wasn't too late.

Chapter 10
DR. KITE

The trek to the grocery store became a scheduled event on Kite's calendar. He marked it in red ink, circling the days Tiffany would be working at the sample meal kiosk. It became a habit, close to an obsession. Somehow it triggered a change in him, energized him, gave him something to look forward to, like a kid looks forward to birthdays, but on a smaller scale. Her schedule became his.

He became more aware of his appearance, how unattended it had become. On a trip to the grocery store, he picked up mouthwash, toothpaste, deodorant, shampoo, shaving cream, a pack of disposable razor cartridges, and plenty of soap.

He made changes. Small, but significant. First, he got a haircut; later he shaved off his scraggly beard. Bit by bit, Kite's life returned as layer upon layer of disarray and neglect was peeled away, replaced with attention and freshness.

The transformation in his appearance spilled over to his habits. He had slacked off on his laundry, throwing a worn shirt and pants over his unwashed body. Now he showered more often and regularly, on a daily basis. His clothes went in the washer after being worn once, instead of strewn all over the floor to be re-worn, sometimes two or three times as he lost track of how many times he'd worn a piece of clothing before it got washed.

Each time he went back to see Tiffany, he peeled off another layer. He became lighter, cleaner, less constrained. His confidence gradually returned.

They established this communication, this routine, as the weeks went by. Tiffany changed too, gradually warming up, paying him compliments when his transformations became a source of pride in his behavior.

The words they exchanged now became less formal, more playful, correlating with his transformation, going way beyond the initial conversation they had, when she'd say, "Hello, sir, would you like to try a sample today?"

"What? You're back. Weren't you here earlier this week on Tuesday and the weeks before that?" Tiffany would say.

"Your menus change each time. I hate to miss one." He'd smile. "Besides, it's become a habit, twice a week, you know."

She'd smile back.

"Hmm," he'd say, stepping closer to look. "What do we have here?"

"Well, today we have savory black-eyed peas."

"Oh, I'll try it," he'd say, reaching for a sample, picking up the miniature spoon from the caddy and digging into the food.

She'd fix her eyes upon him as he ate. She couldn't say what kept her fascinated. To see if he'd enjoy each mouthful, each taste, each texture, or spit it out, disposing the pre-chewed food on a napkin? One thing she knew for sure; he'd give her an honest response.

He'd always finish if the taste test survived beyond the first bite. When done, he'd lick the tiny spoon, carefully placing the spoon inside the cup, dunking it into the trash can nearby. He'd respond to her. A smile or a nod, if it passed. He didn't mince words if it didn't.

She grew to understand his mannerisms, to interpret his pleasure or displeasure without him ever having to say much.

After weeks of variations of the same talk about food, food, and more food, their conversation wandered off the grid. They talked about other things, allowing more hints each time, of their lives, hopes, dreams, and even fears.

Each morsel or tidbit she divulged, shared, gave freely, later became fodder for Kite to relish, to turn over and over, to savor and stretch out until the next encounter.

Kite figured that she didn't realize how much he had changed until, one day, when he spoke to her, when he looked, acted, and had become another person.

Only then did he learn her full name. Tiffany Grant. *Oh yeah, I've got your name. Now, to get your number.*

Chapter 11
ELLEN

The first day passed in a flash. Ellen threw herself into her new job, learning as much as she could. She snapped a picture of her office, the flowers in full bloom, to show her mom.

They celebrated after work. Ellen took her parents out for dinner to the new restaurant she wanted to try. She got a sitter for Angie, someone who came with references, a certification, and first aid training. If this worked out, she'd hire her during the week, a day or two, to give her mom a break.

Ellen's thoughts never strayed far from her baby. Angie was her world now, her whole world.

"Mom, how was Angie today?"

"Angie likes the new picture book you got her. We read it together, and she picks up the words and associations."

"She's learning fast."

"Angie pointed to the picture of the dog today. Said 'dada.'"

"Darn, I missed it!" said Ellen, as a pang of guilt flickered. Being a single mom had its moments, but this sucked, not being able to stay at home with her baby.

"There'll be many more."

"She's a smart one," said Ellen. She was eager to wrap up the dinner and get home.

They ordered dessert to go, a luscious, dark-and-white cake with matching frosting over each half—rich caramel topping drizzled over one side, marshmallows topping the dark chocolate frosting on the other, with a light dusting of crushed nuts over it all.

At the front entrance of her home, she handed the dessert box to her mom and unlocked the door, preparing to greet the babysitter.

"We're home!" said Ellen, shouting over the noise blasting from the TV.

The babysitter was sitting in front of the TV, her feet propped on the table, chips spilling out from an opened bag next to a can of soda. "Oh, hi," she said, her mouth crammed full of chips, hastily chewing. "You're home early. I wasn't expecting you yet."

Ellen laughed. "Angie's in bed?"

"Yeah, she's sleeping," she said. "I gave her a bath and tucked her in." Wiping her greasy fingers on her jeans, she got up, glancing down at the bag of chips.

"You can have them."

"I'm outta here."

"I'll bill pay your account," said Ellen as the babysitter dashed out, headed to her car.

Chapter 12
LILLY

She stood in the middle of the circle, surrounded by women. Pivoting slowly, Lilly looked around, locking eyes with each in a silent greeting. Altogether, an even dozen. An exclusive group. With a satisfied nod, she spoke.

"Welcome to this retreat, a quiet sanctuary away from the rest of the world." She paused to give a brief smile. "My name is Lilly Cooper, and your host for the next two weeks. I know some of you have made a sacrifice to be here, to take this next step in your life. But like anything you endeavor, the outcome is what you put in. I'm here to give you the means. You have to do the rest."

A murmur went around the group, accompanied by a few nods.

"First, a few ground rules. One, turn off electronics. We want you to focus your attention here and do the program. Two, no photos are allowed. Three, you will have to sign a nondisclosure agreement." She paused. "If you don't agree, speak up now."

A hand went up. A thirty-something blonde spoke. "Lilly, what if there's an emergency at home, and someone needs to get hold of you?"

"What's your name?"

"Hanna."

"We have a number for people outside to call. It's on the agreement."

"So they can call in, and we can talk to them?"

"Yes, if it's an emergency."

Hanna sighed in relief. "I read your preliminary guidance in the preparation before coming here. I didn't see a phone number. So we give out this number to people back home before we start?"

"Yes, as soon as you sign the agreement," said Lilly, pointing to a table with two neat piles of papers and a dozen pens laid out. A girl sat behind it. "Naomi will help you out and show you to your rooms. You'll get three meals a day. If you have any dietary restrictions or allergies, please fill out the other form."

A mousy brunette with glasses raised her hand. "I have a question about our rooms. Are we sharing and with whom?" Twisting her head to seek support from the other women, she asked, "I don't know anyone here. How are you going to decide our roommate situation?"

Lilly nodded to Naomi.

Naomi slid out from behind the table. She carried a glass bowl with folded pieces of paper. All eyes focused on her. "I have twelve slips of paper. Each of you will draw a piece of paper from this bowl. On it will be a number from one to twelve." She moved to the middle of the circle. "I'll call out the number one. Whoever has it will call out another number from seven to twelve. The person with that number will be her roommate. I'll repeat this process calling out numbers two through six."

An older woman with streaks of gray in her hair spoke up. "So if you get a number greater than six you don't get to choose?"

"That's right," said Naomi. She raised the glass bowl higher for all to see. A hushed silence settled over the room. "Now, who wants to be the first one to draw?"

Immediately three hands were raised.

"Take one step forward, please," said Naomi. "Each of you will tell the group why you want to be the first. Make it short. We'll go clockwise." She nodded to one woman. "You're first."

"Hi, I'm Geraldine. I'd like to get lucky for once." She didn't elaborate.

A tall woman was next. "I'm Katherine; you can call me Katy." She managed a feeble smile. "This would make my day. By golly, I need it."

The last hand up belonged to the mousy brunette. "I asked the question about the roommates. I deserve to be the first."

Lilly glanced at her watch. "Let's take a vote on who goes first now. You can't vote for yourself. Then we'll draw to decide your rooms. You'll have two hours to unpack and get settled. Be sure to dress comfortably. We'll meet back here for lunch. "

Chapter 13
GIGI

She heard the knock on the front door. She glanced at Rex, still asleep after their late night rousing and lovemaking. Grabbing a T-shirt, she struggled to pull it over her head. Shoving her legs into her jeans, Gigi cursed at the tightness. "Be right there!" she shouted.

Limping as she stumbled, pulling and snapping her pants in place, she hurried to the door. "Who is it?"

"I have a delivery," a male voice replied.

She opened the door a crack, peeking past the taut door chain at the man who stood outside, package in his hand. "I'm not expecting anything. You sure you have the right address?"

"Here," he said, pointing to her name and address on the label.

"What's this?"

"You'll have to sign for it."

Gigi peered at the box, raising her eyebrows at the guy holding it. "Good God, you came all the way out here to the middle of nowhere?" She muttered, repeating to herself. "I'm not expecting this. What could it be?"

"Ma'am, sign here please," he spoke with the measured ease and politeness of someone who's uttered the same words before, many times.

She stared at him, noticing he was barely a man, the boyishness of his face at odds with the starched severity of his uniform. Gigi opened the door, stepped out, and grabbed his pen, scribbling her name. "All done," she said, giving it back to him.

"Thank you," he said, rewarding her with a shy smile, his eyes flickering over her shoulder partly exposed by the T-shirt pulled low, pressing tightly over her breast.

She caught his glimpse and impulsively pushed out her chest, taunting him to have another look. Old habits die hard.

He cleared his throat, moving his eyes away, but not before sneaking another glance.

Bored already with this game, she snatched the box, seeing the red-stamped words, "Handle with care." As he turned around to leave, she uttered a "thank you" to his departing back.

Setting it carefully on the kitchen table, Gigi went to get scissors from the drawer, thinking, *I wonder what's inside.*

Chapter 14
DR. KITE

One day, on what started off as another routine sampling, he grew alarmed when she seemed woozy and unsteady. "Tiffany, you're not your usual self. What's going on? How can I help?"

"I'm not asking for help."

"No, but *I'm* asking," he said firmly.

Kite sprung into action, stepping around the kiosk to reach Tiffany as she braced herself, one hand gripping the edge of the counter. An employee working in the fresh produce section witnessed this and rushed over, offering her help.

"Get the manager," shouted Kite.

"Is she all right?"

"The manager. Now!"

As she hurried off, he turned his attention back to Tiffany. He wrapped his arm around her shoulder, supporting her as she leaned slightly into him.

He whispered, "Tiffany, tell me what's wrong."

"I'm not feeling well."

"Are you sick?"

"I feel dizzy."

He grabbed a bottle of water from the display case behind her cart and gently lowered her with him to sit on the floor, stretching out his legs and holding her head against his chest. With a twist, he uncapped the drink and lowered it, pressing the rim to her lips.

"Here, drink this slowly."

She took a sip.

"We're going to take you to the doctor, find out what's wrong. Okay?"

She gave a slight nod as she swallowed another drink of water.

He took her to the nearest urgent care, accompanying her as the doctor checked her out.

The doctor asked her a series of questions, a history of her medical conditions, what medications she was taking, any other symptoms. With some reluctance, she eventually divulged she was on medication.

"This medication, how many times a day do you take it?" the doctor asked.

"I was taking it three times a day, with meals."

"Was?"

"I mean, but . . ."

"So what do you mean?"

Embarrassed, Tiffany sought support, her eyes pleading.

"Let's start over," said the doctor. "You're still taking this medication?"

She nodded.

"Three times a day?"

"Well, no." She shook her head.

"So how many times a day?"

"Sometimes once a day, or twice."

"So you're not taking this medicine according to the prescription?"

"No," mumbled Tiffany.

"Are you too busy, forgetting to take it?"

Tiffany looked back and forth, from the doctor to Kite. She shook her head in resignation.

"But why?"

"I, um, I wanted to save . . ." gulped Tiffany. "Save money."

The doctor gripped her arm. "Did you decrease your dosage to stretch it out because you can't afford it?"

"I had to," she whispered.

He sighed. "Now you understand the potential danger in not following the dosage."

Chapter 15
DR. KITE

He made sure Tiffany was settled in her home before he grabbed a microwave dinner and headed back to his place.

Splashing cold water on his face, he closed his eyes as it stung his cheeks. Holding his face in his palms, he cradled it. Sighing, he reached for the towel and wiped his face dry.

He sat in a straight-backed chair at the small table, the surface bare except for a cold beer and his tray of microwave dinner. He was still shaken up about the day, and a few things surprised him.

In his mind, he had built up this fantasy about Tiffany. He'd put her on a pedestal and worshipped at her throne twice each week, punctual like the Sunday service and Wednesday nights he remembered from his childhood. She became his savior, one of his own making, but still powerful, as his adoration of her transformed him, as nothing and no one had ever done before.

For years, he had existed in selfish depravity and ruthlessness, caring for no one, driven by his desire for immortality, to change the world—on his terms, at all costs. But when Kite lost it all, he descended into hell, plunging to its depths.

He wallowed in self-pity, ceased to care about anything after the fire burned the warehouse, microchips, computer, and data. And along with these, his inner spirit, his drive . . . perhaps even his blackened, tarred soul.

However recently something had stirred, like green sprouts poking up through the black soil, stirring his feelings for the first time.

Chapter 16
ELLEN

Waiting at the red light, she reached for her travel mug tucked down in the holder beside the driver's seat. Glancing at the clock on her dashboard and the traffic, Ellen figured she'd be at least ten minutes early today, again. Although this new job meant she had farther to travel and needed to get up earlier, the longer drive also gave her more time to think. She ticked off the pluses of this new job like a mantra, repeating the words: "better job, more money, fancy title." All the hard work had paid off. She graduated to this hard-won position.

The cell phone rang as the dashboard screen announced the caller's identity. She pressed the button on her wheel to take the call. "Mom."

"Ellen, I forgot to mention this before you left."

"What?"

"You need to pick up diapers."

"No problem. I'll grab them on my way back. Anything else?"

"We could use more wipes too."

"Okay, Mom."

"What time will you be home?"

"Adding the grocery stop, hmm, I'm guessing around six or seven at the latest," said Ellen. "Will it be a problem?"

"No, tonight's okay, don't be too late."

"Thanks, Mom, you're the best."

Ellen ended the call and settled back in her seat, thinking she had a lot of responsibilities now. Her baby. A new job. Single mom. *She wanted to do it all, and now she'd gotten her wish.*

Chapter 17
GIGI

She slit a line down the center of the box with the tip of the scissors, then threw it on the table and used her hands to rip it open, revealing a gift box and a white card inside. On the envelope, one word: "Gigi." She rubbed her finger across the paper, feeling the raised bump of the letters in her name and the thick, rich texture of the handmade paper.

She read the few words on the card and smiled. Rex. She couldn't help feeling a bit flattered, thinking that he shouldn't have taken the trouble to do this.

She held the gift box, relishing the moment a little longer before carefully untying the ribbon around it. Nestled inside was a case. A gasp escaped her lips as she opened it.

A heart, a ruby jewel necklace, surrounded by diamonds.

She looked toward the bedroom, smiling as she thought of Rex. They had all the time in the world.

Chapter 18
LILLY

Lilly sat in her office, flipping through the forms, counting as she went along. All the women had signed. Touching the sleeve of her expensive business suit, she gave it a slight tug. After today's welcome and opening session, she would ditch it for something comfortable. But for now, she looked every bit a successful businesswoman.

She had put the past behind her, determined to carve out a new life after the nasty divorce. Initially, Lilly allowed herself some time to grieve, to console and feel sorry for herself. It hadn't been easy. She was at her weakest, having used up her energy reserves in the fight for her marriage—only to lose out at the end.

Lilly had fought her inner demons. She choked back the bitterness, the bile rising at those moments of anger. Most of all, she sought to salvage her wounded pride, lamenting the loss of love, the cruelty in which he cast her aside.

She jerked, hearing a knock on the door.

"Lilly, may I come in?"

"Wait a minute," said Lilly. She took the time to compose herself, to wipe the tears from her eyes, before calling out, "Come in."

Naomi poked her head around the door, beaming. "Lunch will be ready in twenty minutes."

"Good." Lilly nodded. "I'll see you there in fifteen."

As the door closed behind Naomi, Lilly opened her purse, searching for the key to the locked compartment. Retrieving it, she inserted the key in the drawer of her desk, the place she kept some files hidden. Lilly flipped back the tips of the file folders, scanning the names on the labels toward the end. The rise of her eyebrow signaled success as she snatched up the file.

Lilly took a deep breath before she opened the manila file folder. With her fingertip, she pushed the paper clip away from the pages, thumbing quickly until she found what she was looking for. She smiled before shutting the file, inserting it back into the drawer in alphabetical order with the name showing on the label. Tiffany.

Chapter 19
LILLY

She joined the buffet line, picking up a plate.

Lilly moved forward as her stomach growled. She took the tongs and dropped two scoops of mixed green salad on her plate, then picked out a sandwich, making a selection from several choices offered, before grabbing a plate with a small wedge of frosted cake. Oh, no sweets, Lilly reminded herself. She tossed her head, heading to the table with the slice in hand. She had cut out the desserts for the most part, but today she made an exception.

When lunch was over, Naomi shepherded the women back into the same room, the chairs now arranged in two rows. This time, Lilly sat behind the table with Naomi. After a nice meal, and the time to unpack and rest a bit, the women were at ease, chatting, getting to know each other better. Lilly nodded to Naomi.

The chime of a triangle got their attention. Lilly stood, walking in front of the table.

"Ladies, I trust you are fully alert and eager to get started."

Quite a few heads nodded, amidst a couple saying, "Yes."

"First, I'd like to welcome you again." Lilly looked around, making sure she had eye contact with each one. "I know many of you have made sacrifices to be here, to clear your schedule, to make arrangements, to be available for the next two weeks." She paused. "Let's remember this. You *wanted* to be here. You *chose* to be here."

The room was quiet. A discrete cough sounded, quickly muffled behind a covered hand.

Lilly continued. "You've all read the paperwork this morning with the details and what we'll be doing, and all of you signed it. There are fourteen days in this program, weekends included. You will be expected to participate every day."

A hand went up, the fingers impatiently waving, determined to catch her attention.

"Hanna, you have a question?"

"Are we going to be graded? I mean, if we work harder, is there some reward?"

"Would it make a difference, working harder?"

She shook her head. "I mean, is this like a class?"

Lilly suppressed the tiniest bit of irritation. "Not in the sense of traditional classes. As you progress through each mile marker, you'll have the self-satisfaction of having succeeded. But I caution you; we'll be watching how you achieve it."

"So how will we know what you'll be looking for?" Hanna persisted.

"There will be set instructions, and there will be

opportunities for you to be creative, to use all of your intellect and resources. Think outside the box."

"Umm," Hanna gulped. "It sounds like you're throwing us a challenge."

"Can I count on you?"

She nodded.

"Are you up for it?" Lilly asked her. Raising her voice, she directed her question again to the whole group. "Are you *all* up for it?"

"Yes," a chorus of voices responded.

"Again!"

This time, the reply was much louder.

Chapter 20
DR. KITE

He awoke, kicking the sheet with his feet. After his tossing and turning all night, the bed was a rumpled mess. He fumbled, reaching for his cell phone to check the time. Four o'clock in the morning. Sighing, he fell back on the pillow, willing sleep to return, but his eyes remained open.

He raised his hand, the one that had cradled Tiffany's head and touched her hair. Ah, what was the scent of her hair? He breathed in and out, trying to recapture the light fragrance. He closed his eyes to recreate the moment in a slow replay.

Inches from her face, he discovered she had a few fine lines, faint but discernible. Her forehead was smooth and noble, and her thick lashes lay on her cheeks like a feather fan, ready to flutter open, revealing her blue eyes. Her nose stood, pert and spunky.

Transfixed by the drop of water clinging to the edge of her lip from the water bottle, he dared not wipe it. He only stared, bent over her. His imagination ran wild. He wondered how many lips had kissed her.

A feeling of power and protectiveness stirred in him as he recognized her vulnerability. The realization sent a surge through him.

In the doctor's office, her revelations had disturbed him just as much as the doctor. It never occurred to him she could be poor and not be taking her meds.

In the early days, Kite had developed a prototype microchip to track medications, to ensure patients took them on time. His initial thoughts focused on the elderly, those with dementia, Alzheimer's, other brain disorders. However, later, he abandoned it for the more glamorous microchips, the ones more appealing to those seeking beauty, weight loss, and health.

Unable to sleep, Kite got up to pace the room, to think. That prototype . . . did he still have the plans somewhere? He had stored the other microchips in the warehouse and their files on the main computer there. But the medication prototype hadn't been kept there, he was sure of it. Fired up now, he opened his laptop on the desk, turning on the lamp.

Sitting and staring at the screen, Kite groaned. Dare he raise his hopes? He searched, his heart beating faster, scrolling quickly. In his paranoia, he had encrypted files and sometimes split them into several locations. Now he'd have to piece them together. As the minutes ticked by, he grew more determined. He was going to find them, no matter what. He had to do this and do this now. A renewed sense of urgency, of importance, took hold. Nothing could deter him at the moment. Tiffany's well-being might depend on it. On *him*.

Chapter 21
ELLEN

She took another look at the presentation, a last-minute check before the meeting this afternoon. A lot was on the line with this first project, this lucrative deal in the making— her new job, Andrew Capstone's trust in her.

"How did I miss it?" she gasped as her eyes caught a typo on the slide, after going over it the *nth* time. Exasperated, she marked the slide and updated the file, making a note to have it replaced in the folder and to alert the presenter. Not a huge error, but to her, it stuck out like a sore thumb.

Ellen glanced at the desk clock. Another hour would give her time to finish up and have a quick lunch in her office while copies were made and updated in all the meeting folders.

She'd be heading to the conference room well ahead of the scheduled meeting time.

She stopped by the bathroom to touch up, applying fresh lipstick and coaxing a few strands of hair back in place. She turned her body, observing it in the mirror, pleased at the way her new suit hugged the curvy outline of her body, accentuating it. She'd kept her weight down after the baby. Tugging the waistline of her size eight pants, she slipped two fingers inside the waistband easily. She felt the looseness, even after lunch. Good. Time for some new clothes, size six.

Ellen walked into the conference room forty-five minutes before 2:00 p.m. She made a visual check. The large wood conference table had been cleaned and polished, the shine and faint lemony smell telltale signs. Name cards were in place, along with meeting folders embossed with the company name on the cover, leather portfolios with writing pads, expensive pens with the company logo, water glasses, and small bowls filled with miniature chocolate bars, handmade by a world-famous chocolatier and express shipped here for the occasion.

The IT guys were quietly working on the opposite side of the room, testing to make sure things worked smoothly. They had installed state-of-the-art equipment Andy had purchased. One of the guys looked up as she walked in.

"Any problems?"

"We're doing the final checks now."

Ellen walked along the table and toward the tall, dark-haired guy. "I haven't met you before. What's your name?"

"Kevin."

"Pleased to meet you. I'm Ellen," she said as she reached out to shake his hand.

"Yes, ma'am."

"Kevin," she said, separating each syllable in his name. "Would you mind running through the presentation for me?"

He nodded, already loading it up.

She pulled back a chair, sitting down. After watching, she was pleased. "Thank you, Kevin." Now she'd leave it up to the presenters to do their job.

Andrew Capstone stuck his head in, his smile widening at the sight of Ellen. "All set?"

"Looks good, boss."

Chapter 22
GIGI

She squirmed, snuggling closer to Rex, feeling the warmth of his body. She spooned him, fitting comfortably into the curves of his body. Gigi rubbed her face against the white cotton of his T-shirt, feeling the soft texture, smelling the masculine scent of the man.

Rex stirred.

She slipped her arm around his chest, her hand brushing his curly chest hair as she reached across to the other side. She thought, *I want to keep holding you like this, babe!*

She thought back to the day they became lovers, unlike Gigi's other relationships. Her beauty was her calling card. The men knew it. She knew it. Those relationships usually started based on pure physical attraction, often at first sight. One guy had proposed to her within minutes, unable to contain himself. She had this effect on men. All men.

In her younger days, she had been a wild child, flitting from man to man like a kid in a candy store. She wasn't in the market for a long-term relationship. Men had come and gone, many showering her with expensive gifts, flowers, fancy dinners, money, jewels—you name it. She had fun; what young girl wouldn't?

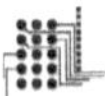

Recently, she had run into someone she once dated. At the time they met, he was already a successful businessman in his mid-thirties.

"Evan?" she asked as he pushed his cart toward her in the store.

He stopped in front of her. "Gigi, how are you?"

"Imagine seeing you." She scrutinized him. Evan appeared a lot older. Still somewhat attractive, but packed with extra pounds and an expanding girth. Perhaps the stress of the job had taken a toll? Maybe he had let himself go, dined on too many rich, calorie-laden meals, slacked off on his exercises? Gotten lazy?

Evan walked around his cart, arms outstretched for a hug. "It's so good to see you!" He seemed genuinely glad.

They had parted on friendly terms. The relationship had fizzled out on its own after the glow faded. Evan moved on, and Gigi did too. But in the time they were together, they sure had fun. They both loved to live it up. He had the money and plenty of it. She made plans, and he went along with it, never squawked about the bill, never stingy, not like some other men.

She pecked him on the cheek before returning his hug. "It's good to see you. How are you?"

"Doing well. I still have the business. Although, I don't travel as much these days. I don't miss it."

"It's been, what, like two or three years?"

He studied her face, a slight frown surfacing on his brow. "You haven't changed a bit." He shifted, peering at the other side of her face, before pronouncing, "Nope, no crow's feet, worry or laugh lines, and not a strand of gray hair."

She laughed. "Don't give me that. It's too early for grays."

"Look at me," he said, pointing at a few streaks at his temples and his waistline. "How do you *not* get this?"

"I must have the right genes," she laughed, shrugging.

"I want some of whatever you're having," he said, half joking, before he straightened up, sucking in his stomach. "You dating anyone now?"

"I am. And it's getting serious."

"Lucky guy," he said, pushing his cart.

As he strolled away down the aisle, Gigi wondered what it'd be like to grow older. How would *she* look?

Chapter 23
DR. KITE

Kite toiled, finishing early in the morning. He lifted his fingers from the keyboard, after finding the files for the prototype chip, occupying space on his laptop. He rubbed his chin, encountering the slight roughness of his stubble while he thought, rejoicing in this stroke of good luck.

In a small packet tucked away in the zip-locked inner pocket of the laptop bag, he had found the tracker microchip, a basic version he had designed earlier to track medications taken. But in his rush to capitalize on his more glamorous, highly profitable chips, this early model had fallen to the wayside.

"Yes!" he shouted. He pushed his chair back from the desk and dashed to the bathroom, acting on the urgency to pee, his bladder screaming out for relief.

He made his way to the kitchen, washed his hands, and started a pot of coffee. Opening the refrigerator, he rummaged through the items on the almost bare shelves, looking for a quick bite. He found a pack of cheese.

Famished, he snatched it, breaking off the pieces, not bothering to slice it. He gobbled it all up, washing the Monterey Jack down with the freshly brewed coffee.

Wiping his mouth with the back of his hand, he leaned on the counter, scanning his small one-bedroom apartment. A forlorn, solitary coffeepot staked a spot on the kitchen counter. A worn armchair faced a twenty-two-inch TV. A desk in the corner. A narrow hallway bathroom with barely enough room to turn. Out of sight was the bedroom, occupied by a twin-size bed, a small table, a makeshift shelf for his clothes, and a laundry basket on the floor, clothes spilling out.

A beam of light filtered through a single window, bits of airborne dust floating in its path as it reached the distressed wood floor.

Kite closed his eyes. Had it come down to this? Would he be able to claw his way back up?

Kite walked across the room and sat at his desk. He caught sight of a pamphlet, partially visible between the papers and tucked inside a larger pocket of the laptop carrier. He flipped through it. Glossy, sexy, like the commercials for drugs treating men who are impotent. First, you see the woman reclined on the bed and your brain links with sex. Enter the man in her life. They have fun together, drinking a glass of wine, sitting in the bathtub, walking together hand in hand, embracing, watching a gorgeous sunset. Fade away.

His fingers probed behind it, in the dark recess of an inner pocket, touching a thumb drive and a foil envelope. He felt the outlines of a capsule as he read the label: "Prototype Number 9." Kite stopped, blood pulsing through his veins.

Trembling and shaking, he carefully opened the sealed packet and peeked inside at the nanobot-coated capsule encasing the new prototype chip. For women and men. Firing up the brain cells and pumping the hormones, orchestrated like a finely tuned piece of machinery, well-oiled and running, all body parts in sync with each other.

But the topping on the cake was its ability to enhance scents—not just any scent, but the most sensual, creating a powerful attraction between a man and woman. A chemical-induced love potion only triggered at the time of implant to capture the unique scents of a man and woman, sending an army of irretrievable nanobots. Multiplied thousandfold. Eros. The ultimate pheromone.

Chapter 24
LILLY

She thought of them as her recruits. Technically they weren't—yet. Not all would make it. This first round of the program would weed out the unfit, the weakest, the least likely to succeed. For those who made it through, it would be the beginning of the real thing. She nodded, brushing aside a nagging thought. Shouldn't she be telling them now?

She'd learned a lot since the first time. She worked relentlessly to put the program together, making changes after the women showed up, fine-tuning it. She started out with six women in the first class. Four women made it through the two-week program. In the end, she offered the next level. Only two women, Tiffany and Naomi, rose to the challenge and finished the advanced level. Tiffany's assignment? Dr. Kite.

Lilly's thoughts shifted to the newly arrived group of women, the second group. They would be stretched to their limits, physically and mentally. Not just a matter of who was the strongest of them all, but also how tough they were, how cunning, relentless, resilient, adaptable.

She had a few select clients lined up, discreetly. Those clients would never meet the women. It was better this way. She took women who looked like the average population, rather than only the fittest and most athletic. For these jobs, she recruited all kinds of women. But only women.

Lilly put her practical business sense to it. By now she had a firmer grip on it, repeating what worked before, discarding what didn't. These women had given up two weeks of their lives to be here. They knew the scope of the program, but only for the two weeks packed with daily body detox routines, fitness and self-defense training, and sessions to push the limits of physical and mental endurance. After they finished, only a few, the best and brightest, would be offered the chance to move on.

She stopped trying to guess. One thing she'd learned was to expect the unexpected.

"Lilly?" Naomi's voice broke through her thoughts. "We have a little problem."

"Already?" Lilly snapped, irritated at being disturbed. "What is it?"

"It's Hanna." She paused. "A message was left for her."

"What did it say?"

"Her mother said her grandmother had taken a turn for the worse. They're gathering the family together." Naomi added, "She sounded worried, distraught, pressed for time."

"When did she call?"

"A few minutes ago."

"Tell Hanna to come to my office please."

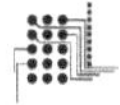

Hanna knocked on the door, entering when Lilly called out.

Seated behind the desk, Lilly gave her a slight nod. Naomi, standing at her side, moved forward to greet Hanna, waving to the empty chair.

"Please sit down."

Hanna hesitated, stepping awkwardly forward. "Am I in trouble?"

"No, not at all. We want to talk to you."

Lilly reached out and pressed a button, replaying the voice mail message from Hanna's mother.

Hanna fidgeted in her chair. "I need to call her back."

"You can," said Lilly. "But you need to decide what you want to do. If you leave the program, you won't be able to come back."

"When do you need my decision?"

"Tomorrow morning, by 10:00 a.m."

Hanna pulled back her chair and stood. "I won't need more time. I've already decided."

Chapter 25
ELLEN

It had been one heck of a day. Ellen looked at the team as they sat around the conference room table and waited for the boss.

Alone in his office, Andrew Capstone tapped his cell phone, ending the call. "Yes!" he shouted. The big Kahuna. He got the contract. Success had eluded him for years. Now he was finally in the big league. His opportunity to swim with the big boys, to get a good exposure on a massive business project, and possibly more work with same guys again in the future.

He leaned back in his chair, fingertips touching. His company, dEsign+, had garnered the coveted project, to interior design and stage the showhomes of Ergon Towers' newest property, the multi-million-dollar condo being built in the swankiest part of town. It would be an expensive project. A lot was riding on showcasing it successfully. Muck it up, and their name would be tarnished.

He pushed back his chair, grabbed his coffee mug, and

walked down the hall to the meeting. His steps were quick and light.

Ellen turned at the sound of the door opening as Andy entered the room.

He set his mug down but remained standing at the head of the table. He surveyed the expectant, upturned faces.

"My father immigrated here at nineteen. All he had in his pockets was some cash his mother stuffed in his hand, money she had saved up. In the old country, he had apprenticed with a master furniture maker at the age of thirteen. When he came here, his dream was to open a furniture store." He paused, recollecting his thoughts. "I remember the first time when he took Mama, my brother, and me to see the place, the building. He wanted to surprise us. He saw beyond the bareness, and it's potential excited him. We had a lot of work to do before the store opened."

He looked around the room, smiling before continuing. "I remember playing there after school. My father called it *his* store—well, technically it was the bank's until he paid it off years later."

Laughter drifted around the room.

Andy put both hands on the edge of the table, leaning forward. "But what impressed me the most was the window display—a white-painted pedestal table set for two, with fine china, glassware, and sterling silverware. Cloth napkins added a classy touch." He looked out the window, thinking back. "My mother came up with this idea. A woman's touch. She even placed fresh-cut flowers on the table. You know what happened?" he asked, raising his eyebrows.

A few heads shook.

"Her display brought in prospective customers. I'll never forget that day, the first day she set it up . . . our store was mobbed."

"Did you work in his store?" someone asked.

"For a while, long enough to know I didn't want the hassle of dealing with inventory. But my older brother, he was made for it." He sighed, standing straight. "I left, went to school, got my degree, and started this company. Now I get to buy furniture and design staging rooms for commercial real estate properties."

"I have something else to share with you," said Andy, throwing a glowing look around the table. "We got the job!" He punctuated his words with emphasis, smiling in triumph, as a round of cheers and applause filled the room.

"Bravo," thundered the man sitting close to Ellen, the sound of his voice piercing her ears.

Ellen caught sight of Andy looking directly at her, flushed with excitement, with the victory. She smiled back, giving him a thumbs-up.

Andy continued to talk, holding his hands up to calm the group. "I want to thank everyone here because *you* did it! Tonight we'll celebrate at O'Brien's Tavern. Tab's on me."

He waited for another round of applause to die down before continuing. "I spoke to an executive at Ergon Towers. They're planning a formal social, an icebreaker, to meet the folks they'll be working with on this project." He waved his hand. "All of you, please mark your calendar for next Saturday night. Any questions?"

"What's the plan going forward?"

"It'll take at least half a dozen meetings to pick cabinets, countertops, fixtures, tiles, toilets, tubs, carpets, color schemes and paint colors. Four model units—a studio, one bedroom, two bedrooms, and three bedrooms—plus an office and reception area. Fully furnished. We'll need to finish first and be in and out of there fast, ahead of sales."

"You all have the packet. Please read it over. We'll meet on Monday morning to outline next steps, flesh out the timeline, iron out some of the issues. Be back here at 9:00 a.m." Andy rose, pausing a moment at Ellen's chair before leaving the room.

Chapter 26
GIGI

The room was dark, curtains drawn over the window. Still, Gigi could make out the shape of his half-curled body on the bed. "Rex . . .?" she murmured, rubbing his back, not sure if he was awake.

He didn't respond.

She moved closer, slipping one arm around his shoulder, nestling her chin to rest at the hollow between his neck and shoulder. She purred, "Honey, are you awake?"

No sound, no movement.

She blew in his ear, knowing how much he liked it, trying to coax him awake. "Rrrrex."

This time, a slight stir, then a shake of the head.

"Rex," she repeated, louder, her hand shaking his shoulder.

"Leave me alone," mumbled Rex, quickly burying his face back in the pillow as he shook his shoulder to shrug off her hand.

"What's wrong?"

Pulling the bed covers up over his ears, Rex leaned away from her.

"Oh, for Pete's sake!" said Gigi. "I don't know what's wrong with you." She bent to grab her clothes strewn on the floor.

Fighting the temptation to go back, she stomped out of the room, making sure to have the last word. "Seriously, Rex, you suck!"

Chapter 27
ELLEN

"May I join you?" said Andy, a drink in one hand.

Ellen looked up, dabbed the napkin on her lips before answering. "Of course, have a seat." She had snagged a small table at the back of the tavern, having joined the party late.

She had been on the phone talking to her mom, making arrangements for her to stay to take care of Angie again. Ellen had promised to give her a heads-up, but this request came in the afternoon, and her mom was not too pleased with the late notice. Ellen had pleaded with her, telling her about the special occasion, an after-work happy hour to celebrate.

When she finally made her way inside the tavern, the party was already in full swing. The dark room of the wood-paneled bar capably held the noise level of a lively, boisterous crowd. She took a few minutes to adjust and locate the rest of the group seated in the crowded, large booths.

Ellen had stopped to greet a few people, making congratulatory remarks as she made her way through the busy tavern, searching for a small table.

Her food had just arrived when Andy stopped by.

"I'm glad you came."

"Yes, well I can only stay for a short while," said Ellen, toying with her napkin. "But I wanted to be here."

He smiled. "We couldn't have done it without your help."

She perked up, taking a celery stalk and dipping it in rich, thick blue cheese dressing, swirling it before taking a bite.

"I liked your story," said Ellen.

"It's true. My father, you would've liked him."

"He passed?"

"A few years ago. My mother is still alive," said Andy.

"And you have a brother?"

"He still runs Dad's company and works there. He never married."

She crunched on the celery.

He watched her lips move.

"Have some," she said, pushing the plate toward him. "This is the juiciest, crisp celery, and the dip is delicious."

"Already had some with my wings."

"I just have celery."

"You didn't order wings?"

"I've changed my diet, cutting out meat. Lots of vegetables, fruits, and nuts."

"Recently?"

"When I found out I was pregnant." She paused. "I made other changes in my life."

He nodded, encouraging her.

"So pregnancy was my inspiration. I was determined to form good habits, to do it right." She paused between another bite of the celery stalk and smiled. "And I feel much better, and healthier."

"Your husband . . ."

"Oh, I'm not married."

"I was going to say he's a lucky man."

She smiled again, looking intently at an imaginary spot on the table.

"I know one thing."

"Oh?" She raised her head.

"You're the best executive assistant I've ever had."

Ellen blushed.

"You don't have to say anything. I want you to know how much I appreciate you." He raised his drink. "Let's have a toast, shall we?"

"I'm not drinking alcohol."

"What are you having?"

"Iced tea." She raised her glass to meet his as his eyes sought hers.

The clink made a pleasant chime. "To us," Andy said, quickly adding, "and to health, happiness, and success."

Chapter 28
DR. KITE

He glanced at his cell phone, willing it to ring, for her to call. He held back from calling her, even though they had exchanged phone numbers after she got home from the doctor's office. He replayed the last exchange they had over and over in his mind—how she looked, what she said, the way she looked at him. He knew something had been communicated between them, a slight spark. He was sure of it.

She didn't protest when he offered to check up on her. But he wouldn't show up at her apartment unannounced. He'd call first. He didn't want to mess anything up, to upset her. She needed to rest last night, so he didn't disturb her.

Once again, he checked the time on his phone. Tiffany had told him today's her day off, and it worked out perfectly after her dizzy spill yesterday for her to stay at home.

Maybe he should take her something to eat? He got up to pace the small room. No longer content to stay there. Itching to take action, to do something for her, for his Tiffany.

Kite picked up his phone. He had already entered her name, number, and address in his contacts. He added her name to his favorites list too. The only name on the list. He called her. Will she pick up on the first ring? Before it goes into voice mail? He pressed the phone against his ear, willing her to answer. It seemed like an eternity, the wait, but in reality, only seconds ticking by.

"Hello."

"Oh," he gushed. "I'm so glad you're there. How are you feeling?"

"Kite? Is that you?" Her voice came across faint, weak.

"Yes, remember yesterday? I said I'd call."

"Ah," she murmured.

"I thought I'd come by, you know, to bring you some food."

"Now's not a good time."

"I'm sorry. I didn't mean to—I thought I'd check in on you."

A pause at the other end, followed by a sigh. "Maybe later."

"Later is good. What time?"

"Hmm, let's see, mid-afternoon perhaps."

"Three o'clock?" He held his ear closer to the phone, hearing something muffled in the background. "Are you there?"

"Yeah, okay," she said before she disconnected.

Five hours. Kite would see Tiffany today.

He rubbed his hands in glee, overcome with excitement. He had time to take a shower, make a list, go shopping and pick up a few items.

He recalled their conversation yesterday when they went to the pharmacy to pick up her medication. She didn't want him to go at first. He insisted on going and paying for it. She relented in the end. She should know better now to take it on time, on schedule, every day. He'd make sure to stress this again when he saw her this afternoon. He straightened up, the doctor in him taking over, switching to thinking of her as his patient now.

He decided to tell her about himself, to reveal what he'd been hiding from her. He had an ulterior motive. He patted his pocket, feeling the outlines of the two injection pens, one holding the tracker medication chip inside and the other the Number 9 microchip.

Would she let him implant the chips? He'd explain. Tell her it'd be for her own good. She'd have total control over how long she wanted it. He would remove it at any time if she told him.

It seemed like forever since he'd seen Tiffany, but only yesterday. Kite checked the time on his cell phone more often than was healthy.

After toweling his hair, he stepped out of the shower and dried his trim body. Although middle age had crept up on him, he'd been careful not to put on too much weight. He wiped the mirror, clearing the fog with his forearm, and studied his face, glimpsing the strong jaw now rid of his beard. He rubbed the five o'clock shadow. Time to get out his shaving cream.

Chapter 29
ELLEN

The week flew by. Ellen was buried in the flurry of activity, working with the team to get the staging design project started. By the week's end, they had worked out a reasonable schedule, outlined tasks, added milestones and deliverable dates.

Andy provided input and guidance when needed as he reviewed the drafts they prepared before approving the document. When Friday rolled around, they met in the conference room again.

"You guys delivered," Andy said as he started off the meeting. He loosened his tie and relaxed, sitting back in the chair. "I know you're looking forward to the social tomorrow, so I'll make this short."

A few nods went around the table.

"I've sent the report. A meeting is being scheduled next week with all parties involved from both companies." He paused. "I got a call, right before this meeting. Unofficial feedback."

Ellen leaned forward. She hadn't heard this part.

"They liked the report. Tomorrow night, at the social, they will announce the managers and introduce the people you'll be working with."

Excited murmurs rippled around the table, and a few shouts.

But Andy wasn't done yet. "I have something for you." He opened his briefcase, retrieved a stack of envelopes labeled with names, and passed them out.

"What's this?" several people asked.

"Go ahead, open it."

Ellen pulled apart the flap, opening the envelope. Around her, the sounds of tearing paper filled the air. She peeked inside, seeing a check. A closer look revealed the number. She gulped, holding the envelope against her chest. A quick look around the table affirmed similar reactions, as a chorus of "Thank yous" sounded, joined by laughter.

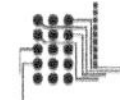

Not bad. The little black dress screamed classy, sexy. Ellen swirled, tossing her shoulder-length hair back. Tonight she'd leave her hair down, the thick brown waves cascading in luxurious layers. She turned, glancing at her side views, feeling the soft tickle of her hair brushing the nape of her neck and shoulder. Feminine. All feminine.

She slipped on her earrings, the long, sparkly ones dangling four inches from her ears. Putting on the finishing touch—a bold pink lipstick—she clicked the case shut. Her manicured fingers dropped the tube in her purse. Ellen took a breath, straightened her dress, and headed to the living room to say goodbye to her mom and baby Angie.

"Wow, Ellen." Mrs. Fulbright's look was admiring, approving.

"Mom, it's my new dress. I'm down to a size six now." Ellen beamed as she preened to show off her figure.

"Your other clothes?"

"I took them down to that place the church opened for women getting back on their feet, getting back to work, The Restocked Closet."

"Sounds like you won't ever need them again."

Ellen shook her head as she reached for the baby in her mom's arms. "Angie!"

The baby gurgled and laughed in her arms.

Ellen hugged her baby and rubbed noses with her. Angie still had a bit of pudginess on her face. Ellen inhaled, catching a faint whiff of the baby's scent, remembering how she loved Angie's new baby smell. Holding Angie's tiny fingers in the palm of her hand, Ellen kissed them. She held Angie close, feeling the warmth of her little body as she lovingly caressed the fine, baby curls on her head.

Angie giggled, her dimpled hand reaching out to pat Ellen's face.

Ellen's mom gave a discreet cough, interrupting as she pointed to the clock.

"I know," said Ellen, reluctant to give up this moment.

"This is your big night."

"Our big night."

"Are you excited?"

"I just want to relax and have fun."

"And Andy?"

"Andy's my boss," Ellen said defensively.

"You've been mentioning his name quite often lately."

"He's *my boss.*"

"That's all he is?"

"I have to go," said Ellen with a departing smile. She gave Angie one more hug before leaving.

Chapter 30
ELLEN

Ergon Towers hosted the social event at the Angora Hotel. One glance told Ellen they spared no expense. The decorations, the singer and the musicians on the stage, the flutes of champagne, the delicate, fancy *hors d'oeuvres* atop of silver plates making their way around the room.

Everyone was dressed up, out to make a good first impression. Even the man with the paunch popping his shirt buttons wore a new suit, a size bigger to contain his sizable girth.

She touched her dress, feeling the expensive, soft material hugging her hips. Well worth every penny.

"Ma'am, would you like one?"

She turned to the waiter and glanced at the champagne glasses. "I believe I will." Ellen reached for a flute.

"Hi," said Andy, appearing suddenly at her side.

Ellen caught her breath. *Who is this gorgeous man?* Indeed not the Andy she knew, her boss, sporting a flattering haircut, dressed impeccably in a slim dark suit, crisp white shirt, and a stunning silk tie.

"You're here," said Andy. He feigned innocence; hiding the fact he'd arrived early, thirty minutes ago, eyes on the entrance, watching for her appearance.

"I'm a few minutes late."

She caught a whiff of his faint masculine scent as she moved closer for the hug. She was unprepared at the pleasing splash he stirred on her senses—the sight, sound, touch, and smell.

"You look amazing," said Andy. He nodded to the waiter before picking up a champagne glass for himself.

"You aren't looking so bad yourself," said Ellen. She touched his lapel in a teasing way. Her fingers traced it to the edge, feeling the smooth fabric. "Good taste." She reinforced her approval with a smile.

"Hey, Ellen," called Jeremy, one of the guys on her team. He was standing with a group of four, gathered in a circle. Three men, one woman. She recognized two of them from her group.

"Come and meet some new folks from Ergon Towers."

She moved away from Andy, walking toward them. Her confidence radiated. She was on top of her game. Their admiring glances bolstered her, and the selection of her dress played no small part.

The circle parted to welcome her. They made small talk, getting to know one another. "I'm Harry," one of them said, peering at her through black-framed glasses.

"Hi, I'm Ellen. Pleased to meet you."

"Enjoying this?" said Harry, waving his hand across the room.

"Nice party here."

"The company likes to do this in grand style."

"You've been with them long?"

"Oh, about eight months," said Harry.

"So you're new."

"Ergon Towers has been expanding and hiring new people."

"Business is good?"

"It's fantastic!"

"What department are you in?" said Ellen.

"Real estate. Condo development and sales."

"Your background?"

"In construction. And yours?"

"I have some interior decorating experience, but my title now is Executive Assistant to the Director," said Ellen.

"You like that kind of work?"

"It's frustrating at times, I'll admit. But you have to be patient and be willing to work with people, see their perspectives, and find solutions."

"Sounds like you have your work cut out for you," said Harry.

"I enjoy working with people," said Ellen, laughing.

"The challenges are there, for sure. But the payoff, when it comes, is tremendous. Our multi-million dollar projects provide jobs not only for the construction industry but many others in the community."

Ellen nodded while enjoying a bite of the smoked salmon with herbed crème fraîche on her plate. "I take it our company is only one among others you'll be working with?"

"Your company is one of the most important. The design showroom is what the public sees. Design it right, and you'll have interested buyers. You offer the vision of a home they admire, want, *have* to have."

"We create curb appeal for the showroom," said Ellen. She paused. "So you'll be our contact on this project?"

"I'll be one of the contacts, as the assistant. My boss is the project manager."

"Is he here tonight?"

He craned his neck to scan the room. Being tall and gangly, he had a better view. "There he is," said Harry. He waved, catching someone's attention, gesturing to him to come over.

Ellen couldn't make him out yet.

Harry nudged her to make room in their circle for the newcomer. Turning to Ellen, he said, "Brad, my boss."

Reaching out to shake his hand, Ellen froze in midair. *Brad? Is it him? Her Brad? The father of her baby?* She hadn't seen Brad since their night together. She hadn't told him about their baby.

Chapter 31
LILLY

She took her red pen and crossed out Hanna's name.

Pushing the folder aside, she called Tiffany.

"Hello?"

"It's Lilly."

"We're making progress," said Tiffany. "He's coming over this afternoon."

"Your medicine, you stopped taking it?"

"Until I got dizzy the other day and the doctor figured it out."

"You feeling better?"

"I'm back on the meds, courtesy of Kite."

"He doesn't suspect?"

"He doesn't have a clue."

"He may be down and out, but remember, he's no dummy."

"Ha! He may be a genius," said Tiffany, laughing. "But he hasn't figured this out. Right now his heart is telling him what he wants."

"The old fool."

"He's not that old. When he's cleaned up, he looks much better."

"But he looked like a bum when you first met him at the grocery store?"

"He *was* a bum, down and out."

"You holding out okay?"

"Yeah, I thought I wouldn't like it here, moving to a small town, leaving the big city."

"And?"

"It slowly grew on me. When I have a day off, I walk along the beach. It's better than medication."

"I'm sorry about your mother."

"I miss her terribly," said Tiffany. She pinched her lips before she bitterly spat out, "She didn't have to die."

Lilly gave her a moment of silence before she spoke again. "I'm very sorry."

"I need time. You know what they say, time heals all wounds."

"Tiffany, I meant to say this, you're like a daughter to me. The daughter I never had." Lilly hesitated. "I don't mean any disrespect. But I'd like to think we're family now."

"I want you to leave me alone too."

"I have since you left the city," said Lilly, thinking about the times she'd picked up her phone and thought of calling her. "I've missed—"

"Enough of this," snapped Tiffany.

"Look, it's a big step forward, what he's doing today, coming to your apartment," said Lilly soothingly.

"No crap. I didn't want Kite to come. But this will move things along much faster."

"Are you sure he doesn't suspect?"

"He thinks I'm a babe waiting for my knight in shining armor," said Tiffany with a hoot. Her laughter faded as she added, "He sounded so disappointed when I first turned him down this morning."

For a moment, Lilly's thoughts flashed back to the night at Duggers, the restaurant where she first met Kite. He was a man of charm, all polished exterior, revealing a glint of the boyish softness inside he tried so well to hide. The man who said to her, 'Tonight is this lady's lucky night,' and '*my* lucky day.' They were both down on their luck that night. She had nothing more to give to him except for a seat at her table.

He paid her attention, listened to each word she uttered, made her laugh, made her forget her pain, gave her hope, made her *want* to live again, to fight her way back to life instead of giving up on it, on herself. She clung to the hope, fixated on it, desperate for the prototype mind-control chip, his magic bullet for all her troubles. She finally called Kite, and he implanted the chip.

She believed Kite when he offered her a way out, an end to the bitterness left behind by her divorce, by another man who took her for all he could, then discarded her, casting her away in one fell swoop without another glance. The infidelity, the betrayal, the baby he had with the other woman, all were egregious. But it was the cruelty wrought by someone she loved, trusted, and devoted her life to that hurt the most, and being reduced to nothing, not even an afterthought. She shook her head to banish her past.

"Be careful," Lilly told Tiffany. "He may seem like a fool,

an old fool. But don't ever let down your guard."

Tiffany snorted and coughed as she tried to catch her breath. "You haven't seen him like this. Men! Such fools!"

"He might try to inject you with his chips."

"What? I thought you said everything burned up in the warehouse fire?"

"You never know. What if Kite's got some stashed elsewhere, like hidden?"

"I'll be careful. I mean, Kite's already paid for my medication, and I'm supposed to be getting better. There's nothing he can do. So if all he wants is to see me for a few minutes this afternoon, I'll play along with it."

"I don't trust men," said Lilly.

Chapter 32
GIGI

They say pretty girls have trouble showing love, giving love. She'd known beautiful girls like that. She was one of them.

Gigi poured steaming coffee into the mug. Her fingers curled around the ceramic handle while with her other hand she rubbed the smooth glaze. She sipped, testing the temperature.

She replayed the scene with Rex. In all the time she'd known him, he'd never acted this way—turned his back on her in bed. Correction. In the *short time* since they'd started sleeping together. Okay, they'd been friends for a long time. They'd only been intimate for a little more than three months. She frowned. *Aren't they still in the bloom, in the rosy period?*

Everything had been great up to this point. Rex had surprised her with this trip. *He's so sweet and romantic,* she thought. She took a long sip of coffee and peeked down the hallway to the bedroom. No sight of him yet.

On the airplane, he had the window seat. Rex had flipped the armrest up and scooted her closer, lifting her legs over his lap, hugging her all during the flight. The stewardess had left them alone.

She had been so excited about seeing this little piece of heaven in the mountains. God's country, wildlife roaming the land. Transported to this place—the city became a distant memory. She could stay here in this idyllic, beautiful land.

Back to Rex. If only she could recapture the magic of the first three months; it had been better than any relationship she ever had. Even though her body went through the motions—the hugs, kisses, the whispered sweet nothings on the pillow, the sex—she had held back. She didn't fake it. She did it willingly. But she wasn't *all* in.

In her past relationships, the men were so grateful for her, the most beautiful and perfect girl they could have, and they were willing to settle for half a heart or less. Her relationships never lasted for long, and when they ended, she did feel sad. Sad not because of a broken heart although sometimes it felt that way, but sorry for the ending. For every beginning, there was an ending in the circle of life. Rex was there to comfort her, to get her through, to make it all better. She never had to wait long, never had a shortage of men.

Rex, he was different. She knew it. As her lover, he wanted her, all of her. Body, heart, and soul. Gigi sighed, feeling the warmth of the mug, wanting more, wanting his warmth again. Could she give him her all?

Chapter 33
ELLEN

Her hands shook, and she tipped her plate, sliding the appetizer right off onto her dress. Turning to Brad, she mumbled a "Hi, pleased to meet you" greeting before dashing off to the ladies' room to get a towel and wipe her dress. No one was at the sink. Ellen put out her hands, leaning against the counter, steadying herself for a moment. *Did he recognize her?* It was the last place she'd expected to run into Brad. She hadn't thought of him for a long time.

He looked great, even better than she remembered. Her stomach fluttered. A flicker of memory popped up, uninvited. Brad naked. The taste of his mouth. The feel of his tongue on her lips, pressing and insistent. Their legs intertwined. She suppressed it, fought it.

The flushing of a toilet interrupted her thoughts. She moved toward the last stall, the large handicapped one with a sink. Grabbing a paper towel, she wet it and wiped her dress, careful not to make it worse. Alone where she wouldn't have to face Brad, she steadied her nerves. She splashed some water on her face, thinking back to the conversation with her mother when she'd asked, "Does Brad know?" *No, she never told him about the baby.* After the night when they had sex, she had wrapped the sheet around her and ran out of the bedroom. She stayed locked up in the bathroom for a long time, not coming out until she was sure he had left.

He had called her. But she didn't answer. He had texted her. She didn't respond. He came to her home and knocked. She didn't open the door. Eventually, he'd stopped.

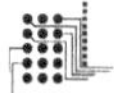

She spun around, surveying her dress in the mirror. The small damp spot where she'd wiped was barely noticeable. She pulled her shoulders up, turned around, and marched out of the bathroom.

"Ellen!" Brad called out from where he was casually standing a few feet away from the bathroom door.

"You remember me," said Ellen cautiously as she walked toward him.

"I wasn't sure at first, but the guys told me your name," said Brad. He stepped closer to her. "You're looking great." He smiled and looked around. "Is there a quiet place we can talk for a few minutes?"

"I noticed some empty meeting rooms. We can go to one of them." Ellen led the way. Down the hallway, they found a small room with a few rows of chairs and a podium, which was vacant at the moment.

"This'll do," said Brad as he plopped down in a front-row chair and gestured to Ellen.

"Brad."

"You left me hanging." He got right to the point.

"Long story."

"What the hell happened? I opened my eyes, and you were gone."

"I . . ."

"Don't you remember?"

"Which part?" Ellen couldn't resist a tease, even as her voice cracked. "The restaurant?"

"You damn well know what I meant!"

"I'm sorry I didn't return your calls."

"The night we had sex," Brad said and paused. "You remember, don't you?" He persisted. "My eyes were still closed, but all of a sudden your body changed . . . You became heavier, and larger like you gained weight. When I opened my eyes, you were gone. Locked yourself in the bathroom."

Ellen was silent. The moment she'd dreaded had come. She struggled to get the words out, but couldn't. Her hand gripped the arm of the chair; the skin stretched tightly over her knuckles.

He walked to a table with a pitcher of ice water and a row of stacked glasses. As he poured, the cubes tumbled into the glass. "Drink this," he said.

"Thanks," said Ellen, shooting him a grateful look. She took a long gulp, the ice hitting her teeth, the cold water rushing past, traveling down her throat.

"Feel better?"

She nodded. "I owe you an apology." She mustered a weak smile. "It felt crazy scary. I locked myself in the bathroom. I looked in the mirror. Realized I was back to my size."

Brad frowned, shaking his head. "I'm confused. So you gained back your weight?"

"Every pound of it and more," said Ellen.

"I don't understand. How could it have happened so quickly?"

"You see, I got an implant, a microchip, and lost weight. I was given a deadline to make good on the offer before the time expired." She spread her hands, palms up in a pleading gesture. "I missed my deadline, 8:30 p.m. that night, while we were having sex. I didn't pay, so the chip expired, and my weight reverted."

"Wait, you got implanted with a microchip? What did it do?"

"It adjusted my metabolism to what I ate. It worked on a cellular level, regulating the mitochondria."

"So it worked, right? When I met you, you were slim."

"Yes, but?"

"But why did you gain your weight back all of a sudden?"

"I knew in the back of my mind it was too good to be true."

"So you had no idea?" Brad persisted, trying to understand.

"Well, yes and no." Ellen paused. "I was given a one-time offer of a free trial period."

"And then what happened?"

"It had an expiration date and time." Ellen licked her lips, which suddenly seemed dry. She took a drink of the ice water before she continued. "I had to pay before it expired."

It finally dawned on Brad. "Let me guess . . . It expired when we were having sex."

Ellen nodded, whispering, "Yes."

"You figured it out then?"

"No, later, after I had cried my heart out and calmed down." She shot Brad an imploring look. "But I couldn't face you, so I took the easy way out."

"I worried about you, but you cut me off." He snapped.

"I'm sorry."

"I thought I'd done something to make you mad."

"I couldn't face you—you would have freaked out if you saw me," said Ellen, brushing a wisp of hair off her forehead. She had practiced multiple scenes, each a bit different, of how she'd tell him, what she'd say if they ever met. She knew she had waited too long.

"Why didn't you call me later?" Brad insisted. "It's been over a year. Did you think to pick up the phone at any time to call me? You had my number. You could have texted me, left me a message. Anything." Agitated, he stood up, pacing back and forth.

"Brad." Her well-planned speeches melted by the wayside. Her excuses seemed pathetic. She thought, *Should I come clean now? When I'm face to face with him?*

Something in her voice, her tone, her look, grabbed him. Brad stopped pacing.

"Please. Please, sit down. I'm not finished yet," said

Ellen. She made her decision.

Brad stared at her, thinking, *What else hasn't she told me?*

"There is something else you need to know."

He was curious. "Tell me everything now." He waited. A muscle twitched in his cheek as he clenched his teeth.

"Brad, you're a father."

"*What?*" He spat out the word, stunned.

"The time we were together, the *one time* . . . I became pregnant."

"A baby—" Brad's mouth dropped open.

"*Our* baby, Brad."

"Boy or girl?" he whispered.

"A girl, Angie."

"You named her Angie." He choked up.

"Yes," Ellen whispered.

"I'm a . . . father" stammered Brad, stopping to soak it all in. He sank into the seat. His head was spinning, flooded with a mixture of emotions—anger, confusion, shock.

Ellen recalled the moment she found out she was pregnant, alone in her bathroom with the test strips. *A single mom,* she'd thought. She had wept. Scared to face the future, wondering if she was cut out to be a mom. She didn't ask for it, hadn't expected it. She'd crawled back into bed, under the comfort and safety of the covers.

She stayed in bed all day. She slept, cried, and slept again. Ellen stared at the ceiling when she woke and cried again. She placed her hand over her belly, moving across the flatness until it stilled, resting over the life she carried inside.

Chapter 34
DR. KITE

Three o'clock. Kite stood in front of Tiffany's door. He pushed his shoulders back, balancing the bags he carried to reach out and ring the bell.

"Coming," said a faint voice from inside.

He waited, fixing a smile on his face.

The door flung open.

He moved forward, eager to thrust the bouquet of fragrant roses toward her. His smile was beaming.

"What's this?" said Tiffany, surprised.

"Get well flowers," said Kite.

"Come on in while I get them in water."

Kite relaxed. Carrying the bags, he followed her into the kitchen and set them on the counter. "I bought some groceries and take-out food," said Kite, quickly adding, "for when you feel like eating."

Tiffany filled a vase, plunked in the long-stemmed flowers, and stooped to smell the roses. "These are lovely."

Kite beamed.

"Let me put the groceries away, and then I'll make a pot of coffee. Would you like a cup?"

"Oh yes, and there's some vanilla biscotti to go with it," said Kite, gesturing toward the groceries.

Tiffany grabbed a plate from the cabinet and pushed it toward him. "Here, you put those on the plate while I finish what I'm doing."

Kite couldn't help thinking, *This is a sliver of domestic heaven. Dare I hope?* He snuck a few glances at her while she wasn't looking. She was the picture of casual chic, the kind he saw in magazines while flipping the pages at the checkout line. Seemingly without effort, she managed to be elegant yet comfy casual, exuding warmness yet keeping her distance. Her beauty was quite remarkable.

He suddenly became awkward, his palms sweaty.

"Hey, you okay?" Her voice close to his ear startled him.

He nodded.

"Thought your mind had gone with that blank look," said Tiffany, propelling him toward the living room sofa. "You sure you don't want something else?"

"I'm okay with the biscotti and coffee."

She hovered over him, fussed a bit to make sure he was comfortable.

He patted his coat pocket, making sure the injection pens were in place. He'd brought both of the chips, the one for the medication reminders, and the other one—for love.

Chapter 35
GIGI

She took another spoonful of the sinfully rich ice cream loaded with chocolate bits, nuts, and caramel swirls. Gigi had grabbed the container and flipped open the lid, eating straight from the cardboard carton. Her go-to comfort food, any time of the day.

She barely looked up when Rex appeared, dressed in a white T-shirt and blue jeans. She quickly shoved more ice cream into her mouth.

"Leaving some for me?" said Rex.

She tipped it toward him, showing the almost empty carton, then scooped up the last bit of ice cream. Licking her lips, she smacked them for emphasis as she finished. She plunked the spoon in the carton and walked to the sink, tossing them both in.

Rex had an urge to shake her, to punish her for her childish act. The clink of the metal as the spoon spilled into the sink sounded loud in the quiet kitchen. But he couldn't deny his part in it. Brushing her off in bed this morning earned him this. Man up.

"Is this our first fight?"

"You could say that."

"We need to talk," said Rex. He dragged another chair beside her.

She got up to fill her coffee mug, taking her time with it before sitting down again.

Rex shifted in his seat. "I'm sorry about this morning."

Her icy gaze was unforgiving.

He twisted to face her. "I haven't been honest with you."

Gigi jabbed her finger in his chest, making sure he could feel her nail. "You turned your back on me."

"I was doubled over in pain."

She stopped pressing her nail and drew back her hand in midair, cocking her head to one side. "You . . . you're sick?"

He nodded, his gaze holding hers. "I didn't want to spoil this trip. I thought I could hide it—until afterward."

"So this morning?" She let out a long breath out, grappling with this.

"Yeah. I had overexerted myself. My body reacted. I was in pain."

"How . . . how long has it been?" Gigi whispered.

"It's recent."

"What's wrong?"

He shrugged. "I went to see a doctor before we left. He drew my blood and ordered some tests."

"So you don't know the results yet?"

"I'll find out soon. I've got an appointment after we get back."

"I'm so sorry," said Gigi as her eyes moistened. She thought, *How can I have acted so shamefully, so selfishly?*

Epilogue

Chapter 36
GIGI

Gigi moved closer to stand in front of Rex, still in his chair at the kitchen counter. Her thighs pressed into his knees as she leaned in, gazing into his eyes. Silently she pleaded forgiveness and at the same time expressed affection and concern.

He wiped the dampness at the corner of her eye with his thumb. As he gazed at her face, his heart beat faster, pumping fresh oxygen into his bloodstream, bringing renewed energy, dulling the pain for a moment. His knees parted, arms raised to wrap her in his embrace.

"I love you, Gigi," said Rex. His voice cracked. He buried his head in her long hair.

"I love you too," said Gigi. She hadn't been put to the test yet, but having said it felt reassuring and gave it teeth. Would she have the strength to support him?

Her thoughts churned back to the times when he was her rock—when she was ill, the car accident, her nightmares.

Gigi stiffened, pulling back to look at Rex, as her thoughts twirled back to the past. The day Rex picked her up at the Hotel Seven, frantic, after searching for her all night when she didn't come home. Her memory was fuzzy after the car accident. Rex had called his friend, Steve Cosine, for help. Steve was a consultant and sometimes a private investigator who retired from the force. He'd found her car abandoned near the Highway 15 underpass after the accident.

"Rex?" snapped Gigi as these thoughts triggered her memory. Back to earlier, when she glimpsed the email—why she'd rushed outside to tell him.

She made an abrupt turn, hurrying back to the bedroom to retrieve the laptop. Carrying it to the kitchen, she set it on the counter and opened it. A few days ago, Rex had insisted on exchanging email passwords in case something happened. She had thought it odd at the time, but it made sense now—his illness.

She clicked on the mail icon and waited for it to load up. "I came outside that morning to tell you something."

"When I was chopping wood," said Rex, nodding. "What was it?"

"An email. The subject line caught my attention."

"Did you read it?"

"No, I ran to get you," said Gigi, shaking her head. "Something about my accident. In your inbox."

She peered, staring intently at the screen as she scrolled through the messages until she found it.

She stopped, pushing the laptop toward Rex.

She pointed to the still unopened email.

He paused.

"Go ahead," Gigi urged him.

Rex clicked open the email from his buddy Steve, the private investigator. He read the one sentence out loud.

Gigi grabbed his hands, stifling a wave of fear as an episode of her life, one she tried to forget, came back to haunt her.

From: Steve Cosine
To: Rex Masden
Subject: GIGI'S Accident - Important Information

We have a match on fingerprints taken from the van used to transport Gigi to Hotel Seven.
Steve

Chapter 37
ELLEN

It was ten o'clock when she made it home. She had texted her mom.

Ellen kicked off her shoes as she stepped in the doorway. Her mom was still up, watching TV, laughing at an old *I Love Lucy* re-run.

"Hi, Mom."

"How did it go?"

"I'll tell you in a minute. I want to check on Angie first."

She opened the door to Angie's room. The baby was sleeping, snug in her bed. Ellen walked in, her bare feet not making a sound. She smiled, staying there a few minutes, watching Angie sleep, listening to her gentle snores.

When Ellen returned to the living room, her mom had turned off the TV and was waiting for her.

"I can tell something happened tonight," said her mom. She patted the couch. "Come, sit down and talk to me."

No longer a child, Ellen asserted herself as a thirty-six-year-old woman. "I don't want to hear any criticisms from you. I've had enough tonight," said Ellen as she sat next to her mom on the couch. Close, but not touching. "I saw Brad tonight."

"Brad? You mean Angie's father?"

Ellen nodded. "Surprise of my life. At the social, I met people from the company who hired us for their real estate properties. One of the guys introduced me to his manager, who I'll be working with."

"And it's Brad?"

"Yup. I froze. I spilled food on my dress and ran into the ladies room to clean up. He was outside, waiting when I walked out."

"No escaping this time."

"He made sure of it," said Ellen. "So we talked. He was angry at first. He had a right to be. I behaved badly. So I told him about the microchip, why I didn't, *couldn't* face him." She paused. "He had a lot to soak in, but I told him more."

"About Angie?"

"Yes, about our baby."

"Was it the right decision?"

"I went with my gut feeling at the moment. Brad's the baby's father."

"Wait, did you lie to me?" She paused. "You told me Brad was out of the picture. You led me to believe he knew about Angie but chose not to be part of Angie's life."

"I didn't say that."

"Which is it?" she scoffed. "I want the truth, not any pathetic lies."

"Mom, I didn't lie," cried Ellen.

"You're angry. Please calm down."

"No, *you* listen to me. I don't want you to interrupt," said Ellen. "How would you know how I feel? Huh?" She stuck her chin out. "And how scared I was when I found out I was pregnant. I was clueless. I doubted myself, wondered if I could do it."

Ellen patted her stomach. "It seemed unreal in the beginning. My stomach showed no signs for weeks. But one day I felt life, knew for sure my baby was alive." She closed her eyes to recapture the moment. "I knew, when I felt my baby kick me. It became the turning point, changed my life. I became focused on becoming a mother, the best I could be, for my baby. I started loving the pregnancy. The idea of being a single mom took root firmly. I became proud of it. Protective of my baby. I relished the rest of my pregnancy. I laughed. I cried hopeful, happy tears."

"But you—"

"I made excuses. I didn't have the guts to pick up the phone and call him," said Ellen. She crossed her arms and straightened up on the couch. "I had the chance to tell him face to face tonight. I made the decision."

"How did Brad take it?"

"He was overwhelmed. Caught off guard. Didn't see it coming."

"How did you feel?"

"Nervous, but honestly, I'm glad I did. I couldn't have picked a better moment to tell Brad. What perfect timing."

"So what did you guys—"

"We are taking baby steps, Mom."

"And the next step?"

"He wants to meet Angie. I've invited him here."

"When?"

"Tomorrow. Brad's going to get back to me about the time."

"You think he'll follow through after he's had some time to think about it?"

"It's up to him. I gave him my phone number and address again, in case he doesn't have it anymore."

"You've done all you can."

"Now it's up to Brad."

Chapter 38
LILLY

The call from Tiffany never came. Lilly kept the cell phone on her all afternoon just in case. By early evening, she still hadn't heard from her. She called Naomi.

"Naomi, I need your help," said Lilly. "Something is wrong."

"Did you talk to Tiffany?"

"Couldn't get hold of her."

A pause at the other end. "I'm worried," said Naomi.

"She was supposed to meet him at three."

"What happened when you tried calling her?"

"It went straight to voicemail."

"I'm going to drive over there. Should arrive by ten, ten thirty at the latest."

"Be careful," said Lilly. *Something must have happened to Tiffany. Why hasn't she called?*

Chapter 39
DR. KITE

He loved dipping biscotti in his steaming mug full of coffee, and dip he did, not realizing how hungry he was. Kite had been excited about seeing Tiffany again and forgot to eat. Laughing to hide the rumble in his stomach, he snatched another one.

Tiffany finished hers and sat back to watch Kite. She plopped both feet on the edge of the coffee table, feeling the stretch.

"When was the last time you ate a proper meal?"

"Oh, if you counted a microwave dinner last night?"

"No," said Tiffany, planting her feet on the floor now, giving a stomp. "I mean a home-cooked meal."

He shook his head. "I, um . . ."

"If you had to think so hard—."

"Do you remember the first time we met?"

Tiffany's eyes widened. She remembered the day when he first came to the store. She had learned how to make chili when they gave her a card with the recipe printed on it. The first batch she'd messed up. She had to pitch it and start over.

"Because I remember every detail," said Kite.

Tiffany suppressed a response. She had caught sight of him hanging beyond the circle of people crowding around her kiosk. His scruffy appearance, the rumpled clothes. How could she not remember? Was he looking for the closest thing he had to a home-cooked meal that day?

Kite was sitting on her couch now, smiling at her, his cheeks clean-shaven, teeth freshly brushed with peppermint toothpaste. His face, childlike in its eagerness, upturned toward her. The change was more than physical. Something deep inside, the child in him, had surfaced.

"When I was in college, I had a part-time job as a nurse's aide at the rehab center," said Kite. "We took care of men and women. The patients, grateful to have help, didn't complain. The staff, we helped each other out." Kite dabbed his mouth with a napkin, wiping away some imaginary crumbs.

"You liked the work?"

"I didn't hate it. The older patients were nice to me. A few of them called me 'young man' instead of my name."

Tiffany smiled.

"The first time I took care of a female patient and washed her, it unnerved me." His fingers traced the rim of his mug. "I had never seen an old woman naked before, and well, I was unprepared for the sight of her sagging breasts, flabby, hanging down toward her waist, the wrinkled skin on her abdomen."

"You bathed women as well as men?"

"Yes, but we respect the patient's dignity when we do it."

"How so?"

"We keep as much of the body covered as possible. As we wash each area—like the arm, leg, chest—only that part is visible while the rest of the body remains covered."

Tiffany nodded.

He frowned, rubbing his chin. "In the operating room half a dozen people may see patients naked, but if no one tells the patients about it, they'll never know."

Kite sighed. "When you die, your naked body lies on a cold stainless slab, exposed in front of strangers in a morgue or funeral home—until it's covered up. And there's nothing you can do about it."

Tiffany clutched the bottom of her cotton plaid shirt, leaving wrinkles as she unwound her fingers. "I never thought of it that way."

He pushed away his empty plate. "One time I walked a patient down the hall, a bit of exercise. Suddenly he grabbed my arm, retching, as he bent over to vomit."

"Where? In the hallway?"

"I didn't have anything close at hand, not even a wastebasket."

"Did you yell for help?"

"There wasn't time," said Kite.

"So what did you do?"

"I caught the vomit midstream."

Tiffany squealed and made a face. "How did you do it?"

"I cupped my hands," said Kite, holding his hands together, palms up, to demonstrate.

"I couldn't do it, not in a million years." She shook her head. For a moment, the hard glint in her eyes softened.

Kite pulled out the pen from his pocket. The one loaded with the chip to keep track of medications.

"What's this?"

"It's an injection pen, loaded with a microchip."

Tiffany frowned, looking at Kite warily.

"Yesterday, you became dizzy in the store, and I took you to see the doctor. You hadn't been taking your medication."

She opened her mouth to speak, but he cut her off.

"This is a prototype chip to track medications. Something I developed a while back, but it got put on the back burner."

"I've got my medication now. Don't need it."

"It'll help you to take your medication on time."

"How will it do that?"

"It will let us know when you've skipped, and when you're late."

"Oh, wait. It'll let *you* know?"

"Yes, both of us. And you'll never have to worry. I'll do all the worrying for you."

"How so?"

"I've programmed it to send out a reminder on your cell phone."

"This is kinda elaborate. Unnecessary, if you ask me."

"If you don't like it, I can take it out, anytime."

Tiffany stared at the pen, slowly shaking her head. "I don't know."

Kite pulled out the other pen, the one with the Number

9 chip. "I have something else. It will set the mood, make you feel better. Make love, not hate."

Tiffany looked from one pen to the other. "But they look the same to me. How do you tell them apart?"

Kite laughed. He pointed to a mark on the side of the Number 9 pen. "This is how I know." He held one in each hand. "Now which one will it be?"

THE END of Book 2

Author's note

Since writing "Alterations" as a standalone, I've heard from readers who wanted the story to continue and suggested a series. I hope you've enjoyed reading book two. It doesn't end here, not just yet. There will be one more. A trilogy.

So thank you, dear readers.

Acknowledgments

To my loved ones, thank you for all your support and good cheer.

Thanks to my fantastic beta readers and Polgarus Studios and everyone who has been a part of this book, in one way or another.

www.ingramcontent.com/pod-product-compliance
Lightning Source LLC
Chambersburg PA
CBHW030211130726
47898CB00012B/982

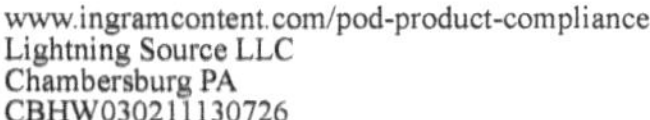